What Has Spots?

Mary Elizabeth Salzmann

Lake Forest
Media Center

ABDO
Publishing Company

Published by ABDO Publishing Company, 8000 West 78th Street, Edina,
Minnesota 55439. Copyright © 2008 by Abdo Consulting Group, Inc.
International copyrights reserved in all countries. No part of this book may
be reproduced in any form without written permission from the publisher.
Super SandCastle™ is a trademark and logo of ABDO Publishing Company.

Printed in the United States.

Credits
Editor: Pam Price
Content Developer: Nancy Tuminelly
Cover and Interior Design and Production: Mighty Media
Photo Credits: Shutterstock, Steve Wewerka

Library of Congress Cataloging-in-Publication Data

Salzmann, Mary Elizabeth, 1968-

 What has spots? / Mary Elizabeth Salzmann.

   p. cm. -- (Creature features)

 ISBN 978-1-59928-872-7

 1. Animals--Color--Juvenile literature. 2. Camouflage (Biology)--Juvenile literature.
I. Title.

 QL767.S247 2007

 591.47'2--dc22

                      2007010189

Super SandCastle™ books are created by a team of professional educators,
reading specialists, and content developers around five essential components—
phonemic awareness, phonics, vocabulary, text comprehension, and fluency—
to assist young readers as they develop reading skills and strategies and increase
their general knowledge. All books are written, reviewed, and leveled for guided
reading, early reading intervention, and Accelerated Reader® programs for use
in shared, guided, and independent reading and writing activities to support a
balanced approach to literacy instruction.

About SUPER SANDCASTLE™

Bigger Books for Emerging Readers
Grades PreK–3

Created for library, classroom, and at-home use,
Super SandCastle™ books support and engage young
readers as they develop and build literacy skills and will
increase their general knowledge about the world around
them. Super SandCastle™ books are part of SandCastle™,
the leading PreK–3 imprint for emerging and beginning
readers. Super SandCastle™ features a larger trim size
for more reading fun.

Let Us Know
Super SandCastle™ would like to hear your
stories about reading this book. What was
your favorite page? Was there something
hard that you needed help with? Share the
ups and downs of learning to read. We want
to hear from you! Send us an e-mail.

sandcastle@abdopublishing.com

Contact us for a complete list of SandCastle™,
Super SandCastle™, and other nonfiction and fiction titles
from ABDO Publishing Company.

www.abdopublishing.com • 8000 West 78th Street
Edina, MN 55439 • 800-800-1312 • 952-831-1632 fax

Many creatures have spots. Their spots can be different colors, shapes, and sizes.

Dalmatians have spots.

Dalmatians are born white. The spots start appearing when the puppies are one to two weeks old.

Leopards have spots.

The spots on leopards are called rosettes. Leopards that live in deserts usually have pale yellow fur. Leopards that live in grasslands, mountains, or forests often have darker coats.

Monarch butterflies have spots.

All monarch butterflies have spots on the edges of their wings. Only male monarchs have two black spots in the middle of their back wings.

Loons have spots.

In the summer, loons are black and white with spots on their backs and wings. In the winter, they molt and turn grayish brown. They don't have spots in winter.

Cows have spots.

Holstein cows are white with either black or red spots. Every Holstein cow's pattern of spots is unique.

14

Giraffes have spots.

Giraffes have brown spots. The spots on a giraffe's head and legs are smaller than those on its neck and body. Giraffes have spots everywhere except their stomachs.

16

Ladybugs have spots.

Ladybugs are a kind of beetle. They are red or orange with black spots. A ladybug's spots fade as it gets older.

Fallow deer have spots.

Most fawns are born with spots, which disappear as the deer grow up. The fallow deer is the only deer species in which the adults have spots.

Moray eels have spots.

Moray eels live in tropical oceans. There are about 200 species of moray eels, and most of them have spots. Morays can even have spots inside their mouths!

What would you do if you had spots?

MORE CREATURES
THAT HAVE SPOTS

hyena

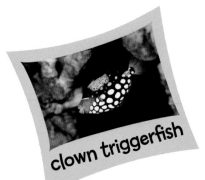
clown triggerfish

cheetah

moth

green tree python

GLOSSARY

creature - a living being, especially an animal or insect.

develop - to grow or change over time.

fawn - a young deer.

grassland - a large area of land covered with grasses.

male - being of the sex that can father babies. Fathers are male.

molt - to periodically shed feathers, fur, or another outer covering.

pale - light in color.

pattern - a combination of characteristics that repeat in a recognizable way.

species - a group of related living beings.

tropical - located in the hottest areas on earth.

unique - the only one of its kind.